LONGM

M000233990

Frankenstein

Mary Shelley

Simplified by John Turvey
Illustrated by Per Dahlberg

Longman

Longman Group UK Limited,
Longman House, Burnt Mill, Harlow,
Essex CM20 2JE, England
and Associated Companies throughout the world.

This simplified edition © Longman Group UK Limited 1988

First published 1988

ISBN 0-582-54154-9

Set in 10/13 point Linotron 202 Versailles
Produced by Longman Group (FE) Limited
Printed in Hong Kong

Acknowledgements

The cover background is a wallpaper design called NUAGE,
courtesy of Osborne and Little plc.

Stage 3: 1300 word vocabulary

Please look under *New words* at the back of this book
for explanations of words outside this stage.

Contents

Introduction

Mary Shelley

Mary Shelley was born in 1797. Her father, William Godwin, was a thinker and writer who believed – and you will see that this is important in his daughter's novel *Frankenstein* – that men and women are by nature good. It is only what they are taught and the way they are treated, he wrote, that makes people evil.

Mary's mother died when she was born. She, too, was a writer. Her main subject was the rights of women, and she was a great fighter for those rights – at a time when a woman needed great courage to make such a fight.

Mary married the poet Percy Bysshe Shelley when his first wife died in 1816. They spent the summer of that year in Switzerland.

It was one of those summers that Europe sometimes suffers: rain, rain, and more rain. Shelley and his wife and their friend Lord Byron, another poet, had to find ways of passing the wet days. One way of amusing themselves and each other was to write ghost stories. We are not quite sure how serious they were about these stories. Certainly ghost stories and stories about mysterious and terrible happenings and evil spirits were popular at the time, but not all readers, or even writers, of such stories were serious about them. Jane Austen had already written (though it was not published until 1818) her *Northanger Abbey* making fun of the "gothic" horror novels about mysterious and frightening doings in ancient castles.

Shelley's and Byron's stories were not published, and we don't know much about them. But Mary Shelley's story about a ghost in Switzerland seemed so good to the two poets that they said: "You ought to make your story into a full-length novel and send it to a publisher."

As she worked on her story, Mary Shelley's ghost became the far more frightening "human" monster that we read about in this book. The book was published in 1818, and it became famous at once. Thanks to films and television, the name of the man, Frankenstein, who made the monster, is known all over the world today, and many fearful imaginary creatures are said to be like Frankenstein's Monster.

Frankenstein

People read *Frankenstein* as a story of fear and danger, but Mary Shelley expressed in it beliefs that were important to her and to many of her friends. She believed, like her father, that human beings are naturally good. They become evil only because society – the way men live together – makes them lie and cheat and behave badly. In Mary Shelley's book, Frankenstein has tried to create "the perfect man", with strength, beauty and a clever brain. When life is given to his "perfect man", there is great strength and a very good brain, and he is naturally good. But he is ugly – so ugly that people fear and hate him. He looks evil, and so society treats him as evil. The result is that he actually becomes evil, an evil being of great strength and cleverness, bringing danger not only to Frankenstein but to Frankenstein's family and to those he loves. Mary Shelley wanted to show that the evil was not in the Monster at first; it grew because people were stupid, unfair and cruel. Society produced the dangerous Monster instead of the perfect man. Frankenstein himself started the trouble: he drove away the creature that he had made.

Some of the places that are named in this book are tourist centres today. People fly to Geneva. They take a train up from Chamonix to the Mer de Glace glacier. But when Mary Shelley was in Switzerland there were no planes and no trains. Travel over the steep Swiss roads was by horse-drawn carriage, and it was slow and not at all comfortable.

We ought perhaps to remember one other fact. Frankenstein's experiments with the power of lightning were suggested to Mary Shelley by some experiments of Benjamin Franklin, the American scientist and political leader. In 1752, during a thunderstorm, Franklin flew a kite with a key tied to the string near the ground. When he touched the key, it sparked and he could feel an electric shock. The next two men who tried this very dangerous experiment were killed.

Chapter 1
The young Frankenstein

My name is Henri Clerval, and I was born in the city of Geneva in 1775. My closest friend at school in Geneva was Victor Frankenstein.

The Frankensteins were a rich merchant family, and my friend's father had travelled widely. On my first visit to their house in Geneva, I saw a rather pretty girl, perhaps a year younger than us.

"That's my sister," Victor said. "Or rather, we've been brought up together and we think of each other as brother and sister. She is, in fact, Italian."

The Frankensteins were Swiss.

Victor explained. "Soon after I was born, my parents were in Italy. On a very hot day they asked for a drink at a farm. They saw five small children there. Four had dark hair like the farmer and his wife; one had fair hair and looked quite different. That was Elizabeth, the daughter of a landowner who had lost his life trying to free his country from an unjust government. My mother was not strong; it was not certain that she would have another child, but she did want a daughter. She asked the poor farmer and his wife if she could take Elizabeth and bring her up as her own. In the end, that was arranged."

"It's like a story from a book," I said. "You are lucky to have a sister. I have no one to talk to at home."

Frankenstein smiled. "Then she must become your sister, too."

Elizabeth did become a sister to me, and remained a sister all the time that we were children. All three of us belonged to each other.

Besides the fine house in Geneva, the Frankensteins had a country house on the south side of the lake. They liked the quiet life there, and they lived there more and more after the birth of another son. They called him William, and a happy country girl of our age, called Justine, came to look after him. These were the people among whom I spent more and more of my time.

From the beginning, Victor Frankenstein's interests lay in science. He studied nature with a kind of hunger, seeing the world around him as so many secrets to be discovered. There were secrets in the deep waters of the lake, in the mountains, in the glaciers – the great rivers of ice that flowed down from the mountains – and in the changes of weather and season. As a boy, he always wanted quick results from his experiments, but Elizabeth and I enjoyed helping him with them.

I remember a day when we were out collecting wild plants for one of those experiments. We had come down from the long, low mountain called the Salève, and we were crossing a field near a line of fruit trees when a thunderstorm broke. We were getting very wet in the open field, but we knew the danger of standing under trees in a thunderstorm.

Suddenly there was a noise like a gun, and a flash of blue light, and we were thrown to the ground, blinded and unable to hear. When at last we were able to see and hear again, we saw nearby the remains of a tree, black and smoking. It had been struck by lightning. The power of that lightning was something that we could never forget.

It was from that day, I think, that an idea began to form in Victor Frankenstein's mind.

It was decided that Frankenstein should go, at the age of

Lightning strikes the tree

seventeen, to study science at the University of Ingolstadt in Germany. His father thought highly of a professor of science there, Dr Krempe. I, too, wanted to go to a university, but my father would not agree to my going. He could only see laziness, drinking and wasting time in the student life.

Before Frankenstein left for Ingolstadt, there was a very sad happening for all of us. His mother had never been very strong. She fell ill, and it soon became clear that she was not going to live. She called Victor and Elizabeth to her bedside. Joining their hands together, she said:

"Victor, my dear, I hoped to see you and Elizabeth married. Promise me that your father will live to see it."

She died soon after.

I did not see Frankenstein for two years after he went to Ingolstadt. Nor did his family. We received letters from him at first, but these became fewer and shorter and told us less.

Chapter 2
What Frankenstein had made

About September of the following year, his letters stopped completely. He did not come home to Geneva for holidays, and I could see that his father and Elizabeth were troubled. In his last letter he said that he had learned as much as Ingolstadt could teach him. If this was true, then what was it still kept him there?

Even a letter to Krempe brought a reply that added little to what they knew. Frankenstein had indeed left the university – against Krempe's wishes – and was now following some studies of his own (though what these studies were, Krempe did not say).

Eight months passed without any news, and then old Frankenstein decided to act.

"Somebody must go to Ingolstadt. It cannot be me. My travelling days are over, and Elizabeth cannot give up her duties in the house. We shall have to arrange something," he said, giving me a look full of meaning.

Soon after this, old Frankenstein appeared at my house and asked to see my father. My father, as I have said, was a hard man, but old Frankenstein was good at making people change their ideas. The fact that he was rich and an important man also helped my father to allow the following arrangement to take place. In return for help with the cost of my studies I would go to Ingolstadt, where I would enter the university and find out what Victor was doing. Having found out, I was to look after him if necessary, and to make him write home.

So it happened that because my friend stopped writing letters I was able to escape from my father's shop and do what I wanted to do above all things – to go to university.

The very next day I took the public carriage from Geneva to Lausanne and from there to Berne. It was a four day journey across Switzerland to Lake Constance, then into south Germany by Ulm to Ingolstadt.

It was late afternoon when the carriage crossed the River Danube and entered the walls of that pleasant old town, then washed in the golden light of late summer. That, at least, is how it must have appeared to me that first time. But when I think of what happened later – when I think of what first saw the light in that little town, I cannot remember Ingolstadt without feelings of pain and horror.

I left my bags at the inn where the carriage stopped and asked my way to the street where my friend was staying. Number sixteen was one of those fine old houses, built a very long time ago, that one still finds in those south German towns. I climbed up four lots of stairs until the only other stairs were those that led up to the roof. There was just one door with a card pinned to it. It was dark there, but I could read the name: Victor Frankenstein.

I moved my hand down the side of the door until I found the bell, and pulled. A long way inside I heard it ring. As I stood there listening to the sound of footsteps coming nearer and nearer I wondered what changes two years had made in my friend. Two years is a long time in the life of a young man.

The footsteps reached the door, and I heard the sound of several locks being turned – it seemed as if he kept his door very carefully closed. At last it opened, and there he stood – Frankenstein! Yes, it was him, but not the Frankenstein I remembered. Deathly pale, with wild eyes and an uncared-for beard, he was not the young man who had lived the healthy, out-of-door life with me in the mountains

Frankenstein opens his door to Henri

of our own country. This thin body on which the clothes hung as if they had been made for someone bigger could not have walked five kilometres. I wondered if he ever left his room.

However, I found no cause for displeasure in the way he received me. After a moment of surprise he came forward and took my hand. A look of joy appeared on his face.

"Henri," he cried, "you come just at the right time."

He drew me inside, and then closed the door. This took some time since there were, as I had thought, several large locks. Visitors were clearly neither expected nor wished for.

Frankenstein led the way down a long, dark passage to a book-filled room. A bed stood on one side, looking as if nothing had been done to it for days; and on a table near the window were the remains of several meals. There was dust everywhere, and the last of the evening sun shone with difficulty through the dirty windows. There was a rather unpleasant smell.

After I had given him news about his family and told him the reasons for my coming to Ingolstadt, Frankenstein got up and walked about the room excitedly. He did not seem to be thinking at all about what I had just told him.

"Henri," he said at last. "You have come just at the very moment when I need your help. The great work which I have been doing for the last year is coming to an end, and I shall soon know whether I have been wasting my time or whether I have pushed scientific discovery to new heights." His eyes burned with a strange light. They were like the eyes of a madman.

"My preparations are nearly complete. All I need now

are the right conditions for the great experiment to take place.

"Come," he said, and led the way to a door in a corner of his living room. "You will see what no other man has seen."

He threw open the door, and at once the strange smell which I had noticed before became stronger. It was like the smell of bad meat. I could hardly bear it, but my friend seemed not to notice it, and led the way in.

The room was dark, and at first I could only see a mass of wires, glass bottles and jars, and copper and glass pipes. Here and there the blue light of burners made holes in the darkness. And from those places the sound of boiling liquids could be heard.

As my eyes began to see better in the half-darkness I saw that this stuff was arranged round some kind of bath in the middle of the room with a wooden work-table that went all the way round it. Frankenstein was watching me. There was still this strange excitement in his eyes.

"Go on," he said, "look inside. See what I have made."

I bent over the table and looked into the bath. It was filled with a clear liquid. I tried to see deeper into this liquid, but at first all I could see was what looked like hair – fine hair. I bent lower, and as Frankenstein moved a lamp nearer I drew in my breath sharply. It *was* hair – spread out in a golden ring around a face, a head. More. Yes, there was a body in the bath – the body of a man!

The body in the bath

Chapter 3
Creating life

Back in the living room I sat down at the table with the wildest thoughts racing through my mind. As Frankenstein sat down opposite me he looked in the lamplight even thinner and paler than before. His eyes still shone in an unnatural way, and his hands would not keep still. Was he mad? Was the man in the bath someone he had killed? For the first time in my life, I think, I feared him.

Then he began to speak – in sudden flows of words which stopped, and then started again. I began to understand two things: first, that he had hardly spoken to anyone for months; and secondly, that there was only one subject which he was able to think about. He spoke at first of his studies at the university, of his early experiments, and how little by little he found himself spending more time in his own rooms than listening to his teachers. But it was clear that he could hardly wait to pass on to the one subject that filled his mind.

"... and so, the science of living bodies became my chief study – the science of life, and the science of death. It seemed wrong to me that we knew so much about all those activities of the human body that make up life; and yet we did not know how those activities can be set in movement. To me a human body is like a clock. Sometimes a clock stops; the spring has not run down, and all the little wheels are there. But it stops. What do we do? We pick it up and shake it, and nearly always it starts again. So I asked myself two questions: first, how does one make a human body, and secondly, how does one 'shake' it into life?"

11

"You mean, create life?" I said.

"Yes, create life." Frankenstein looked at me with a kind of smile. "That is an idea which does not please you, I see."

"No, it does not please me," I replied. "It is not for man to create life. There are things which man should not try to know or do. Man has his proper place in nature, and it is better that he should not try to move out of it," I said.

"My dear Henri," Frankenstein replied, "if man had always believed that, there would today be no science, no learning. Have you never thought of the great difference between what man could be and what he is? Have you never looked at man in the streets and then looked at man in the paintings of the great artists? If you had the power to create, would you not want to create the perfect man?"

"If?" I cried, thinking of the body in the bath. "You know quite well that you have already created a body. Do you think you have the power to give it life?"

Frankenstein did not answer. He got up and walked to the window and opened it. It had been a hot day, and there was no air in the room. In the distance could be heard the sound of thunder.

"This is our season of storms," he said, and looked out of the window for some minutes. Then he turned and went on speaking: "The man of science has no more power than any other man. Any power more than his own must be taken from nature. In the next few days you will see what nature and I can do." He looked hard at me. "You could even help me."

Help him? Was he asking me to help him create life? Although I felt horror at his suggestion I also knew that my friend was offering me part of the honour which success could bring. But would the experiment succeed? And – more important – did I really want it to succeed? As I

12

watched Frankenstein's shaking hand and the sudden, strange movements of his face, I wondered again if he was just a little mad. I felt a wish to leave Ingolstadt at once, until I remembered that I had been sent there by his father to look after him. It was my duty to stay.

In the days that followed, the more I thought about the experiment the more it seemed a kind of madness. Could I really join Frankenstein in an act that was against nature, God and man?

I could, and did. My reasons for doing so were quite simple. This mad plan of his could not possibly succeed. And when it failed, as it certainly would fail, it would be my duty to look after my friend, and help him in his sorrow.

I moved into Frankenstein's rooms, and the first thing I did was to create order and cleanliness, and to make sure that he ate meals at the proper times. Next, I did my best to understand the nature of his discoveries. This was hard, since I was not, like him, a man of science; and if I had been, it might still have been difficult. Even I could see that he had gone far beyond what was known to science at that time. He tried to tell me, but I never did understand, and I ended up simply doing what he told me to do.

It was not, in fact, understanding that I needed most in my work for Frankenstein, but strength of mind. I had to work in a room filled with jars containing every part of the human body: arms, legs, hearts, everything. This was quite disgusting to me, but Frankenstein seemed quite untroubled by it, and picked up these human parts as coolly as a woman in the kitchen picks up a piece of meat.

"In order to get what I need for my work," he said, "I have had to go to hospital, the prison, and even the place where dead bodies are put into the ground. To create life I

13

have had to live side by side with death."

But it was not the eye-balls which stared at me from inside the jar as I entered the room; or the brain lying in its clear liquid like some strange sea-creature; or the carefully cut off hands waiting for something to get hold of that really troubled me. It was the centre of it all – the long, white bath where "he" lay.

I often used to think as we worked that "he" was asleep, and that we and our doings were part of his dream. Or was it that I was asleep, and that he and Frankenstein and that room were part of mine? At first it was all so strange. But as the days passed I began to lose my fear of him. After all, this was to be the perfect man, and Frankenstein had chosen his parts well. Certainly he had strength and beauty. More than two metres tall, and with that long, golden hair, he appeared more than human. Of the brain that slept behind those closed eyes I knew nothing, but Frankenstein was quite sure that its powers would be no less than the strength of his body.

I had only one doubt.

"So," I said one day, while we were sitting eating in the living room, "strength, beauty and cleverness will be his. But what about goodness? Does that perfection which you plan for him go so far?"

"It is all prepared," said Frankenstein in reply. "I have plans to take him to live in a place far from the spoiling example of man, where training will bring out his natural goodness. Man is always born good. Evil can only come from man's bad treatment of man. Treat him justly and he will be good."

I could not answer this. It was what I, too, believed, and for the first time my mind began to enter the world of Frankenstein's hopes and dreams. Suppose, after all, that the dream came true. The body was complete. Could the life-force be made to enter into it?

As if he knew my unspoken thoughts, Frankenstein then spoke: "I am now ready. I am only waiting for the right conditions." He went across to the window and opened it. Again I heard the sound of thunder.

"We shall not have long to wait," he said.

Chapter 4
We seem to fail

The next day was hot and the air was heavy. A storm was on the way. Dark clouds gathered in the sky, and by late afternoon it had started to rain in big drops.

All that day Frankenstein had been excited. He seemed to want the storm to come. It was as if he had a place for it in his plans; and as the rain fell faster and faster and the thunder grew louder and louder, he became more and more excited, walking restlessly up and down in front of the open window.

About seven o'clock he suddenly seemed to decide about something. He shut the window and marched into the work-room. I had by this time caught his excitement myself. It was clear that the experiment was about to begin. But when he reappeared a few minutes later my surprise was so great that I started to laugh. He was carrying a child's kite.

"Are we going to play games, then, Victor?" I asked at last.

But my friend remained quite serious and said nothing. Instead of the excitement of a few minutes ago his face now wore the fixed look of someone who knew exactly what he had to do.

I followed him along the passage to the front door, and up the stairs that led to the roof – or rather, to a flat but narrow part of it that lay between two high, pointed parts. On the right I could see a lighted window set in the roof just below its highest point. That must be the window of Frankenstein's work-room.

It was dark and wet, and the wind was very strong. I

held the kite while Frankenstein climbed up to the window, which, I noticed, was a little open. I saw him pass his hand through the opening, and in less than a minute he was standing by my side again with the end of a piece of wire in his hand. I then noticed that there was also a roll of thin wire tied to the kite. He joined the kite wire to the wire which came through the window, and then took the kite from me.

I was glad of this, because the wind was pulling at it all the time, and I was afraid that it would carry me off the roof and into the street, five floors below.

But Frankenstein was too deeply interested in what he was doing to feel fear. Holding the end of the kite in his teeth he climbed up to the window again, and from there to the top of the roof. He sat there with one leg on each side of the roof.

"Up you come, then, Henri," he called. "I need you."

I followed him up, and he put the kite back into my hands.

"Move along to the other end of the roof and sit facing the wind. I will hold the wire," he said.

When we were boys we had loved flying kites; and as I sat there in the wind and the rain an unexpected feeling of pleasure ran through me. I lost all my fear of falling. I could see in the lightning flashes that Frankenstein was smiling. He felt the same as I did. It was a game now, and playing it made him feel as if he was a child again. I think it was the last time I ever saw him as happy as he was then.

I held the kite up and let the wind take it. Little by little Frankenstein pulled it up into the stormy night. Higher and higher it went, and still the wire ran out through the work-room window. When he thought it had gone far enough, he tied the wire to something just inside the window. Then we climbed down from the roof and returned to the house.

Frankenstein had never forgotten the power of lightning. The picture of that blackened tree below the Salève had stuck in both our minds from the time that we were boys. But while I remembered the lightning as a destroyer, Frankenstein had seen further. For him it was a power for creation. Now he was going to try out that power.

At any moment the kite would sail into the very heart of the thundercloud, and a huge electric force would flow down the wire into the work-room. To give life? I still could not believe it.

As we sat silent in the living room listening to the thunder coming nearer and nearer I thought of the perfect man lying in his bath in the next room. Sleeping? Dead? Unborn? I did not know how to think of him. But I saw the lightning flashes and I forgot him then. I was too afraid of the lightning. Did Frankenstein know what he was doing in drawing down lightning on the house in this way? He could not know the force with which the lightning would strike. He had an arrangement for leading the electricity to earth, but would it work? It was like sitting next to a bomb of uncertain size, waiting for it to explode.

When it came, of course, I was unprepared. There was a huge noise, a flash, and everything went dark.

It seemed like an age, but it can only have been a minute later when I woke up. I could not hear because of the explosion; nor could I see. I thought at first I had been blinded by the flash, but I soon understood that our lamps had been blown out. I could also smell burning. Frankenstein's earth arrangement had not worked too well, and a great part of the force of the lightning had hit the work-room.

Frankenstein and Henri go into the work-room

Frankenstein was already on his feet and making his way to the room. The door had been blown open by the explosion and was only just hanging from the door post. Inside was darkness and an even stronger smell of burning. As we entered we felt broken glass under our feet – and other things that were unpleasantly soft.

The surprise of the lightning had made me forget everything, and it was only when my hands touched the table in the centre of the room that I remembered the experiment. But Frankenstein had not forgotten. He was already bending over the bath, feeling inside with his hands. A distant flash of lightning lit up the room just long enough for me to see a blackened table, a broken bath and the body lying face downwards in a few centimetres of liquid. It was quite still.

"The experiment has failed," said Frankenstein, and led the way out of the room.

It was the end of all his hopes, and I felt deeply sorry for him. Yet, though I could not say so then, it seemed that things had happened in the best possible way. I had never really wanted it to succeed.

By then, very tired, we threw ourselves down on our beds without even taking the trouble to undress. Before the storm had passed we were deeply asleep.

Chapter 5
The Monster

Even though we were tired, too much had happened that night for us to sleep with easy minds. I had dreams – dreams of strange things coming to life on the work-room floor. I dreamed of Elizabeth walking through the streets of Ingolstadt. Pleased and surprised to see her there I walked up to her and kissed her. But as I took my lips away I saw her lips turn from red to the blue-green colour of death. It started to spread across her face, and I forced myself to wake up.

This must have been about half-past four, because I remember the church clock striking the half-hour soon afterwards. I sat up in bed and drew the back of my hand across my face, which was wet with fear and horror.

I looked round. The curtains were closed, and everything was very dark. There was no more thunder, and the storm had passed. My eyes fell upon the open doorway leading to the work-room. It was dark like everywhere else, but less dark, since a little light came in through the window in the roof. As I sat up in bed thinking of the clearing-up we should have to do when daylight came, a shadow moved into the lighter darkness of the doorway. The shadow became a shape. It filled the doorway and then left it empty again. It had passed into the room where I was. My blood ran cold. Something was standing very close to my bed.

Then I heard a sound from the other bed. Frankenstein was also awake. He suddenly pulled the curtains open, and the unkind, grey light of early morning flowed into the room to show – what can I say? I could see at once that it

21

The shape in the bedroom

was the body in the bath, now alive and breathing. But where was the perfection? Where was the man-god of Frankenstein's dreams? Was this the end of the great experiment?

There he stood, unclothed, wet and shining, his long hair hanging down over his chest. If he had stood up straight he would have been a giant – as it was, he was nearly two metres tall – but his back was bent, and his arms hung in front of him like those of a huge monkey. As for his face, the beauty of the body in the bath had gone with the lightning. Instead of the rosy white of skin before life, the living skin was yellow and dry like old paper, and was stretched across the bones like a piece of clothing that was too small. This left the teeth uncovered, so that he wore an unnatural smile all the time. Lightning burns and lines where the pieces of skin had been joined together marked the rest of his body; and the whites of his narrow eyes were the colour of blood. He was a monster!

No one spoke. The only sound was that of the liquid dropping off the ends of the Monster's hair on to the floor. Frankenstein was filled with horror. He stared at the Monster and the Monster stared back at him. As for me, after the first surprise I felt nothing but plain, simple fear. But as the minutes passed I began to understand that there was no reason for fear. This was not a wild animal. If he had meant to attack us he would already have done so by now. He was no more certain what to do than we were. As he stared in that fixed way at Frankenstein, it almost seemed as if he knew that he was looking at his maker. He even began to look friendly. Did he want to thank the man who had given him life?

Almost as this thought passed through my mind he took a step forward, went down on his knees and stretched out a hand. I think he was going to kiss Frankenstein's foot. But whatever he meant to do, he did not have a chance to do it, because, with a cry of horror, Frankenstein kicked out, and the Monster fell back. He got up very quickly, which showed that although he looked heavy he was strong and active. Now it was his turn to look surprised, and Frankenstein, seeing that the Monster was not as dangerous as he had thought, took his chance. He picked up a heavy stick and stepped forward.

"Out!" he cried. "Out of my rooms! Out of my sight! You are disgusting!"

Still with a look of hurt surprise on his face, and without saying a word, the Monster turned, and Frankenstein ran after him down the passage, where the front door, pulled in by the force of the explosion, lay wide open. He ran out and disappeared down the stairs.

I went straight to the window and looked out. After a minute the Monster came into the street. He seemed uncertain what to do, but in the end he ran off through the still empty town towards the main gate.

"He is disgusting," said Frankenstein. "I cannot bear to think of him."

"But he is yours. You made him," I said.

"He was a mistake."

"Perhaps, but he was *your* mistake. He is yours, and he knows it. Did you not see how he treated you as his master? And what did you do? You drove him away. That was neither good nor wise."

Frankenstein grew pale at my words. His whole body shook. "He is *not* mine. He was a mistake, I tell you – an experiment that went wrong. He is not even human. I owe him nothing!"

"But, my dear fellow, what is going to happen?" I

asked. "You cannot just let him run off like that."

"Nature has made a mistake, and, as Nature always does, she will put her mistake right in her own way. This creature cannot live. You could see it was incomplete. It will die a natural death and there will be no more difficulties."

This did not seem a right and proper answer. I tried again: "But do you not feel you have some duty——?"

"Duty!" cried Frankenstein in an excited voice. "Do not speak to me of duty. I have spent too long in this town wasting my life in useless study. I shall return to Geneva. I shall go back home. Yes, I shall leave today!"

Frankenstein took the carriage to the south that evening. I waited in his rooms, expecting trouble. One does not lose an unclothed monster in a small town like Ingolstadt. When nothing happened, I went to the market to make enquiries.

The Monster had run straight out of the town gates. Only the gatekeeper had seen him, and nobody believed him. "He has been drinking again," they said.

"What luck!" I thought. "Frankenstein was right. The Monster will go into the forest and die."

I began to work very hard on my own studies. I heard nothing from Frankenstein, and there was no news of the Monster.

But in September I was buying food in the market when I heard an old wood-cutter talking about a "wild man" in a certain part of the forest. The next day I walked to that part of the forest.

All that day I talked to people who lived in the forest. It was clear that there was indeed a wild man in the woods, even though nobody had been very near to him. He had done no harm. He had attacked nobody. When anyone saw him, he ran away – and he could run very fast.

I knew that I had to find the Monster. I felt that those who made him owed him something; it was somebody's duty to make friends with him so that he would not turn against the human race.

I spent several Sundays looking for him. At last, from behind a bush, I saw him. He was even more frightful than I remembered, but he had changed. He had found some clothing, and he was carrying a basket full of wild fruit. I decided to follow him. He came to a little wooden house in an open space in the forest, pushed open the door, and went in, still carrying his basket.

About ten minutes later, he came out, but not alone. An old man and a very pretty girl came to the door with him. I saw him talking to them – proof that the Monster could talk.

He went off into the forest again, and after a time I went to the little house. The people in it were French: old de Lacy, who was blind, and his son Felix and daughter Agatha. They had had to leave France because of unjust laws. They were good people who had been kind to the Monster.

"He lives in a little hut behind the house," Agatha said. "He is very strange, and very ugly, but there is goodness in him. He cuts wood for us and gathers wild fruits in the forest."

"Other people in the forest call him 'the wild man'," Felix added, "but he is quite clever. He has learnt French only by listening to us. He also listens when we read to Father, and he now knows a great deal."

"I should like to meet him some time," I said. "Perhaps

Henri sees the Monster go to the little house

he is the former servant of my friend Frankenstein. His master has gone back to Geneva, but he will want to help his servant, and I will write to him."

I still hoped to get Victor to do his duty.

My work, and very bad weather, made it impossible for me to return to the forest for three weeks. When I went back to the little house, nothing remained of it except a few stones and a mass of blackened wood.

I found proof that the de Lacys had died in the fire, but I could not see whether the Monster had died or not.

I went back to Ingolstadt and worked hard, trying to forget. Then in December I received a letter with a cutting from a Geneva newspaper. William Frankenstein, Victor's little brother, had been murdered, and Justine was to be tried for the murder. The story was that Justine took William into some woods and put her hands round his neck until he was dead, and then she ran off with the gold chain from his neck. They caught her at Thonon.

That was just not possible. Justine loved little William, and she was a kind and loving girl. I decided to return to Geneva at once to try to help either her or the Frankensteins.

Chapter 6
Murder!

I arrived in Geneva a few days later at about nine o'clock in the morning. Knowing that the gate would be shut before I could reach the city, I had spent the night before in the nearby town of Nyon. I then took a boat along the north shore of the lake to Geneva.

The place where the ships tied up did not seem very active for the time of the day, but this did not, by itself, surprise me. However, when I passed through the city gates I could no longer fail to notice the emptiness of the streets. It was clear, bright weather for the time of the year, and the hard-working people of the city should all have been at their businesses. But everywhere I looked, shops and offices were closed. Only a little thought was enough to tell me that I had made no mistake about the date. It was not a Sunday or a public holiday.

Soon I noticed another thing. The few people who were in the streets were all going the same way – towards the opposite side of the city, and they were in a hurry. They could only be going to Plainpalais, a piece of flat, open land on the far side of the River Arve where the men of the city, doing their soldier training, used to march up and down on Sunday mornings. It was also – as I remembered with sudden fear – the place of public hangings!

I started to run: across the old market-place, up the street where the city government meets, until, breathless, I joined a large, silent crowd on the city walls. I could see nothing, so I pulled myself up into the window of a house. Below the walls I could see an even larger crowd. All Geneva was there – and more, since there were many

29

people from the small towns and villages around.

In the middle of the crowd was a raised wooden floor with a post in the middle and a rope hanging from the post. Among the few people standing there was a girl in a black dress. Even at that distance I knew it was Justine.

This crowd was not like any other crowd I had ever known. It was somehow strange and frightening that, although so large, it made so little noise. The air was thick with hate. They wanted that poor, frightened girl in black to die, and it was nearly time for her to do so.

As the last prayer was said, and the rope was placed round her neck I jumped down from my place in the window. My eyes filled with tears and I could watch no more. I turned away from the crowd into the peace and quiet of the Rue des Granges. But I had not gone far before I heard a deep cry of pleasure rise from the crowd, and I knew that Justine was no more. I stopped and placed my hand on the wall of a nearby house. Suddenly I felt quite ill.

As I stood there in the empty street trying to gather my thoughts, it came to my mind that the house I was resting against was well known to me. It was the town house of the Frankensteins. I walked on to the front door, which I found a little open. I pushed my way in. There was no servant in the hall, so I called. All was quiet. Had everybody gone to the hanging?

As a close friend of the family I felt free to walk upstairs; and finding the door of my friend's room open, I went in.

At first I thought the room was empty like the rest of the house, but then I saw somebody kneeling in a corner, his face pressed against the wall, and as still and silent as if he were dead.

"Victor!" I called quietly. He made no reply. I began to

The people come to see Justine die

think he really was dead. I got hold of him and pulled him out of his corner. His face was wet with tears. "Victor, it's me, Henri. I have come back from Ingolstadt to help you." He still made neither sound nor movement.

"To help you," I said again.

"I am beyond help," he said at last.

"None of us are beyond help ... except (I could not help adding) ... poor Justine." As I spoke her name Frankenstein let out an unhappy cry.

"I could not help her," he said. "I tried ... God knows how hard I tried, but they would not listen. I told them again and again who had killed William, but I had no proof. In the end they thought I was mad."

"Then it was not Justine who killed him?"

"How could you ever have thought it was? That sweet young girl ..." His voice broke. "You knew her. That is enough."

"Then who did kill him?" I asked.

"Do you need to ask? Why, it was *him*."

"Him?"

"Yes, yes, the one I made and gave life to, who has followed me here to destroy my happiness."

The Monster had followed him here? Had he not died in the fire, then, together with the de Lacys? I began to understand the full horror of what had happened. I had told the de Lacys where Frankenstein lived so that they might tell the Monster. It was my turn now to feel as Frankenstein felt. Was it really because of me that two people who never did anybody any harm had died. To think that I had once felt sorry for this creature. Why, why did I have to search for him in the forest? The thought that I was the cause of so much unhappiness was almost too much to bear.

I had told Frankenstein in my letter about my first visit to the de Lacys. Now I told him again about the fire and their frightful end. That, at least, owed nothing to me. Then I told him how my words to the de Lacys had led the Monster to Geneva.

My friend listened in silence. But it was clear even before he began to speak that he did not think I was the cause of these evils.

"He is devilishly clever," he said. "He would have found his way to us without your help – be sure of that. I know you meant well; but he does not return good for the good actions he receives. I have made something un-changeably evil, and I have not yet learned the full cost of his making."

"Surely," I replied, "all creatures are born with the possibility of becoming good or evil. This monster may yet be changed. Did not the de Lacys' kindness bring out the good in him?"

"Yes, and how did he return their kindness? Do you think that they died by chance? No, they were destroyed by him just as surely as my William was."

I stared at him in horror at the idea. Did he mean that this creature had set light to the house of a family that had made him their friend? I could not believe it. There was no proof. And yet Frankenstein had planted doubt in my mind. If he really had killed William, there was nothing, however evil, that he could not have done. But again – did he murder William? I asked Frankenstein to tell me his story.

"You know," he said, "why I returned to Geneva in August after the failure of my experiment. It was not because I feared the monster I had made, or the people of Ingolstadt. I simply felt I had to escape from a town where

33

I had wasted so much of my life. I knew that it was time to go home.

"For some months I lived happily with my family and began to make plans for further studies. I decided to leave science, and was thinking of studying music. Then one day, quite without warning, my happiness was destroyed for ever.

"Justine and William went out every day when the weather was fine. There was nothing to make us think that this day would be any different from all the other days: nothing in Justine's manner to suggest that she was planning murder. There are two stories about what happened after they left the house, Justine's and the court's. You have, I am sure, heard the court's. Your father must have written to tell you all about it. Now let me tell you Justine's.

"This is how she told it: after leaving home they walked up the hill, as they often did, to a little wood about half a kilometre away. Just before they got to the wood Justine sat down on a rock to do some needlework, while William picked flowers. He must have gone into the wood, because a little later she heard his voice coming from the trees together with another deeper, rougher voice. As she stood up to see who he was with, she heard him give a cry of fear. She ran into the wood and was just in time to see him being carried off under the arm of a huge, ugly, hairy man with no clothes on.

"She tried to pull William away from him, and suc-ceeded for a short time in weakening his hold on the boy. But this only made the man seize William by the neck with one hand, and hold him at arm's length away from Justine. After keeping her off for a time with his other hand, he at last struck her so suddenly and so hard that she fell to the ground. When she woke up she found herself in the same place, and William beside her dead, with black fingermarks on his neck. His broken chain lay nearby. The man had quite disappeared.

"Think how the poor girl must have felt. Would they say it was all because she had let William go off into the wood by himself that he had died? Would they believe her story of a wild man whom nobody had ever seen before? All kinds of thoughts must have been mixed up in her mind; and I can understand why she did not want to go back to the house. So, with the gold chain still in her hand, she made the great mistake of running away. As you know, she got as far as Thonon, where her wild looks and strange manner caught the attention of the authorities. They held her there. Then the news of the murder arrived from Geneva."

"Are you quite sure that the wild man in Justine's story was ... your monster?" I asked.

"I was able to question Justine closely in prison, and what she told me makes me think that he may have changed since you last saw him. You say that in the forest he wore clothes. He now seems to have given up clothes completely, and there has been a growth of hair all over his body. But I have no doubt it is the same creature."

"What did you do when Justine was taken to prison?"

Frankenstein turned pale. "Everything ... everything I could to save her. I would have died in her place at the Plainpalais this morning if they had let me. But the trouble was that the authorities would not believe me. When I started talking about a monster I had made, they thought I was mad. And even if they had believed me, I could not have proved that it was the Monster that had killed William.

35

"I went to the wood, and found marks of feet, but they were not very clear. Besides it rained heavily the next night. So when I showed them to the authorities they said that they meant nothing. In the end I saw that my only hope of saving her was to prove that there really was a monster; and to do this I had to find him. I spent the next three weeks searching the mountains all around, but with no success."

"And Elizabeth?" I asked. "How did she take it?"

"Even without knowing what I knew, she did not believe that Justine was a murderer, and she did what she could to save her. But Justine would not save herself. She seemed to think that she was in some way the cause of William's death, and she no longer wished to live. She did not even try to say anything in her own favour in court. In the end even Elizabeth came to doubt her story."

Frankenstein looked very tired. "You must rest now," I said. "You trouble yourself too much, thinking that they died because of you. They did not."

"It *was* because of me," he replied. "And as for rest, there will be no rest for me until I find and destroy the creature I have made."

Chapter 7
We find the Monster

Frankenstein spent many months looking in the mountains, where he was sure the Monster was hiding. In August he began to search near Mont Blanc. He went to Chamonix near the bottom of the Mer de Glace glacier, the great river of ice coming down from Mont Blanc.

One day we decided to cross the glacier itself. It was dangerous because of the deep cracks in the ice. We had to walk round them, and it took us a long time to reach the rock in the middle of the glacier. So we were surprised to see someone coming very quickly, straight across the ice towards us.

"It's the Monster," said Frankenstein.

The Monster came on until he was about ten metres from us, then stopped. He appeared to be staring at us, but his eyes were so hidden by the dirty hair that hung down over his face that it was difficult to know what he was thinking.

We looked at each other for some minutes in silence. Then he moved nearer, bringing with him a strong animal smell. If he had meant to attack us, he would surely have done so by now.

Instead he began to speak. It was the first time we had heard his voice, which was deep and rough. But the manner of his speaking did not prepare us for what he said. We were surprised to find that behind that voice lay a thinking, feeling person.

"You may wonder why I have come to meet you here," he said, fixing his look upon Frankenstein. "It is not to destroy you, as you would destroy me if you had the power

Frankenstein and Henri see the Monster on the glacier

to do so. It is to tell you my story. When you have heard it, then, perhaps, you will tell me whether I owe anything to you or to any man.

"First let me tell you how I found myself alone, cold, hungry and unclothed in the forest near Ingolstadt. What my life before had been I did not know, except that I remembered being in a room and you looking with disgust at me and shouting.

"I learned quickly how to live in the forest. There were springs for water and wild fruits for food. My stomach learned to take the roughest and poorest food. After all, I was not quite human, as you well know. At first I was cold, and had to walk about at night to keep warm, sleeping during the day when the sun shone. Later I found clothes hanging outside the houses of villagers. I saw what humans wore, and wished to wear the same, since at that time I still foolishly hoped to be received as one of the human race."

The Monster's voice at this point shook with feeling. He went on: "But humans were disgusted by me. One day I decided to enter a village to see what would happen. And what did happen? The children ran away, the women cried out in horror and the men threw stones at me. The body that you gave me disgusted them as it disgusted you. In the end it disgusted me. I decided to go deeper into the forest to die – as you no doubt hoped I would. It was then that I came upon the house of the de Lacys.

"At first I used to watch them from behind the trees. I used to see Felix go off into the forest and return with firewood. I saw the old man sitting in the sun. But when I saw Agatha I put away all thoughts of dying. I thought that she was as much above all the other human beings as I was below them. I wanted to be her friend. I wanted to be a friend to them all. So I began to gather wood in the forest every day and lay it beside their door; and sometimes wild fruits – early in the morning before they got up.

"One morning, just as I was putting the wood there, the door suddenly opened, and there stood Agatha. When she saw me she was surprised and frightened, but she did not shut the door. She gave me food, and I stayed. They all began asking me questions, but I could not answer them then. However, as I visited the house again and again, I began to understand and speak their language. In the end I moved into the little hut behind the house. And when Agatha and Felix used to read to their father in the evenings, I listened, and learned about the world outside the forest. I even learned to read, myself, and learned from history that human beings hardly treated each other any better than they treated me.

"I learned, too, the meaning of words like brother, sister, father and mother. I saw that I had none of these. I could not even remember having been a child. Had I forgotten all my early life, I used to wonder. Or was there nothing to forget? Could it be that I had not been born, but made already fully grown? If so, who had made me? All I could remember was a face. But whose face was it?

"The answer to my question came by chance. A man called at the cottage one day while I was in the forest and talked to the de Lacys about my 'master', Frankenstein, of Geneva. At last I knew my maker's name and where he lived. One day, I decided, I would go and seek him. But before I could do this, something happened which turned me against the human race for ever.

"I saw that in the world people lived in families, but I had no family. I knew that families could be made by two people who loved each other. From the time I first saw her,

Agatha had seemed to me like something from another world; and the longer I lived with the de Lacys the more I grew to love her.

"One day when Felix had gone to the town, and the old father was asleep in his room, I found Agatha reading a book under the apple tree in the garden. I knelt down in front of her and told her of my love. I took her hand and kissed it.

"She pulled it back as if I had laid a red-hot iron there. Without a word she threw down her book and ran into the house. She stayed in her room all that afternoon. She did not have to speak: her face told me everything I needed to know. It had the same look as the first human face I ever saw – a look of horror, fear, disgust.

"I knew then that I could never find happiness in human company, and ran off into the thickest part of the forest. For days I lay there, turning my sorrows over and over in my mind. Why should these humans treat me as they did? Was I just an animal to work for them? They had used me but never loved me.

"It was then that I decided to destroy them. One night when they were all asleep, I came quietly to their house. First I made sure that nobody could get out, by rolling large rocks against the doors. Next I went to the place built into the outside wall of the house where Agatha used to make bread. I blew the dying fire to life again, and with a handful of dried grass I carried the fire to the edge of the roof. The roof was made of dry stuff and burnt easily. I stood aside and waited." The Monster's voice stopped. He closed his eyes and rubbed his hairy body with his great hands. He smiled as he remembered.

"After a time I heard cries from inside. But the windows were small, the old man was blind, and there was

41

The Monster sets fire to the house

thick smoke. They died; I laughed; and ran off into the forest. I was on my way to Geneva.

"I travelled by night so that I should not meet anybody. Because I no longer wished to belong to the human race I gave up wearing clothes, and soon found that the cold did not trouble me any more. Coming down from the mountains to the east end of the Lake of Geneva, I swam across the lake to Savoy, and went on towards Geneva along the south shore.

"At that point I knew I was faced with a difficulty. I knew that Geneva was a large town, and I had no way of finding where my maker lived. But I was lucky. Early one morning as I was passing some large country houses quite a long way before the town, I read, cut in the stone gate-post of one of them, the words *Villa Frankenstein*. I had arrived.

"I spent the next four days in the woods above the house, waiting for you to come walking that way, so that I could speak to you. But you never came. Instead, one afternoon I saw a young woman with a child coming up the path. I did not know who this child was. But as I watched him picking flowers and wandering nearer and nearer the place where I lay, an idea came to me. I would try human company once more. If I could take a child like this, too young to have fixed ideas, it might grow up to love me and be my friend. Yes, I would carry him off to some lonely place in the mountains and bring him up in my way.

"So I waited until the child came into the wood, and then got hold of him. He fought and cried out. The young woman came up and tried to pull him away. I held the child out of her reach; but I was holding him by the neck, and by the time I had dealt with her he was dead.

"I knew I could not stay after that, and so I crossed the

mountains to this place, where I have been living in a cave on the edge of the glacier ever since. I was going to come to you, because I have something to ask you. Instead, you have come to me!

"Yes, Frankenstein, with the strength that you gave me I could kill you now, and your friend as well. But because I need you, I will not. I need you to make my miserable life worth living. Make me happy and I will be good."

At this, Frankenstein, who had remained silent all through the Monster's story, began to show interest. "What do you want?" he asked.

"A wife," the Monster replied.

"A wife?" cried Frankenstein. "Are you mad? Where can I find a woman who would want to be the wife of an evil creature like you?"

"You cannot find one," said the Monster. "That is why I have come to you. You must make me one."

"What!" shouted Frankenstein. "Make another like you?"

"A woman – as ugly as myself."

"Never!" said Frankenstein. "The very idea is so frightful that I will not even think of it. Even if you throw me down the deepest crack in the ice I will never make another like you."

The Monster smiled again his evil smile. "Even if I throw not only you, but all those whom you love down with you? Master, think again. You are putting others in unnecessary danger – your friend here, your father, the young woman who lives in your house. Besides, I am ready to make you a promise. As soon as you have made her we will both leave the world of cities and men, and go to the forests of South America. You will never see or hear from us again."

44

For a time nobody spoke. Then Frankenstein turned to me. "Leave us, Henri," he said. "Go back over the ice and wait for me there. This creature must have an answer."

I wanted to stay, but I could see from Frankenstein's look that he wanted to be left alone. The sun had already gone behind the mountain, and a cold wind began to blow down the glacier.

"Come soon," I said, and started back across the ice. When I looked back they were as I had left them, still talking on the rock while their shadows grew longer.

Chapter 8
Elizabeth

It was an hour before I saw Frankenstein coming back across the glacier. If he had been any later he would have been in danger of losing his way among the cracks. But for the Monster to let him go at all must mean that they had reached an understanding of some kind. He came on so slowly that I could tell what that understanding was. It was not just because he was tired: he brought news that he was unwilling to tell.

"Did you promise?" I asked.

"How could I not have promised? He calls me 'master', but he knows very well who commands and who obeys."

"And if they have children?" I asked. "If they create a new race in South America, enemies of the human race . . . ?"

"I cannot even be sure that he will keep his promise and go to South America," Frankenstein replied. "But that is a chance I have to take. What can I do, Henri? He comes and goes so secretly. His powers are more than human. He will destroy my family if I do not do what he wants. God knows how hateful this is to me, but I cannot do anything else. I just have to make another monster. And . . ." He stopped, as if uncertain how to go on. "And again I shall need your help. Are you willing to give it?"

This was the question I feared. I had done little to help with the first monster. That had been Frankenstein's creation. Would the second monster be not just his, but ours? I did not think it right to make a second one. And yet, if I did not help, and the second monster was not made, I would be leaving the Frankensteins to face certain death.

Also, even after all that had happened, I had to be fair to the Monster. Did he not have a right to happiness? Those words of his kept coming back to me: "Make me happy and I will be good." The mistake had been to make the first monster; but having made it, might Frankenstein not be right to make another?

"I will help you," I said at last, "but only by keeping you supplied with what you need, by keeping you fed, and by carrying letters to and from the place where you work. But I will take no part in the work itself."

"I ask no more," said Frankenstein in reply.

We returned to Belrive the next day. The weather remained fine, and we began once more to live that happy family life which we had almost forgotten. The deaths of Justine and William were still in our minds, but they no longer hung over us like dark clouds. As for Frankenstein's promise to the Monster, he seemed to put it quite out of his mind for the next few weeks. Time passed pleasantly. We went out in the boat, we read in the garden, we went for walks in the hills. We did everything rather than begin work on the new monster. In fact, Frankenstein found so many reasons for waiting that I began to wonder if he would ever begin.

In the end two things moved him to start. First his father called him into his room one day.

"Victor," he said, "you will remember that just before your mother died she told you her greatest wish. I am an old man, and it would please me if before I died I could see that wish come true. It may be that by now you think of Elizabeth more as a sister than as a possible wife. You may even know someone else whom you like better. If so, you must say, because I am not the kind of father who forces his children to marry against their will. Please think about

47

this: if she is not to marry you, we must find somebody else for her. She has a right to know what your feelings are."

Frankenstein knew that his father was right. Elizabeth ought to know how she stood. She had never said a word about marriage, or even let him feel that she was thinking about it. About his own feelings he was quite clear. Yes, he wanted to marry her – he had no doubts about it – but not yet. First he had to carry out his promise to the Monster.

This was one thing that made him decide to begin work. But there was another. Elizabeth was not just a simple housekeeper. She had a quick mind and a woman's natural curiosity. She knew that Frankenstein's unhappiness was not the result of William's and Justine's deaths alone. Something else was troubling him, and she wanted to know what it was. Nor was this just curiosity. She loved my friend, and only wished to learn his secret in order to help him.

However, both Victor and I had always been careful to keep the truth from her. We thought it would do her no good to know, and we did not like it when a most unpleasant happening one night gave her much to think about.

At this time we used to go to bed quite early. There was nothing to stay out of bed for in the country. Besides, Frankenstein did not find it easy to talk to his father and Elizabeth. He had too much to hide, too much that he could only talk about to me. So, one windless, moonless night, a few days after old Frankenstein's talk with his son, Elizabeth lay in bed reading by the light of a candle. Opposite her was the dark square of the open window; and through it from time to time little flying things kept coming in, drawn by the light of her candle.

Elizabeth sees the Monster at her window

She looked up from her book as one of them flew in, and her eye was caught by the appearance of the window. There was something different about its shape – something that had not been there before. She looked again. Two large, brown, hairy hands had appeared at the bottom of the window. As she watched, too frightened to move or speak, the hands turned white as their owner slowly pulled himself up.

Elizabeth was prepared for the face of a thief, but not for this; not for the hanging yellow skin, the watery eyes, the knotted hair and the join lines. She let out a sharp cry, and the face dropped below the window again. The hands disappeared. Less than a minute later I was in her room and listening to her story.

I lit a lamp and went out into the garden. I hurriedly kicked soil over the marks of feet that I found in the soft earth of the flower-bed below Elizabeth's window.

". . . a dream, a bad dream . . ." I could hear Frankenstein saying in the room above.

"I tell you, it was not a dream, Victor," Elizabeth replied, coming to the window. "Can't you see anything down there, Henri?"

"Nothing," I said truthfully. I said nothing about what I *had* seen.

"See," said Frankenstein. "How could anyone put his hands on your window and pull himself up, as you said? It is more than three metres to the ground. Why, a man would have to be unnaturally tall to do such a thing."

Elizabeth said no more. She knew we were trying to hide something, but it was not her way to ask questions. She shut the window, and went back to bed.

Next morning Frankenstein came to my room with the look on his face of a man who has decided on action.

50

"I cannot leave things any longer," he said. "The creature has been watching us for weeks. Last night he must have been trying to find me and went to the wrong window. I know he will not let me alone until I have done what he wants. I cannot take the chance of another visit like last night's. Besides, who knows? Next time it could really be Elizabeth whom he has come to see. I cannot have her frightened like this. We start work at once."

"But you cannot work here," I said. "She already knows that something is going on."

"Exactly. That's why I am going to leave home. In my search for the Monster earlier this year I found by chance an empty wood-cutter's hut in the valley of the Arve. It is far enough from Belrive to make it safe from family visitors, but near enough to Geneva for me to get the supplies I need."

"And my job?" I asked.

"It will be better if you stay here most of the time," he replied. "But you will visit me often, bringing food and letters." He stopped and thought for a minute. "There is another thing I want you to do ..."

I looked at him expectantly.

"If, for any reason, I fail to complete this work, it may not be me who will suffer first, but Elizabeth. Guard her, and be prepared for anything."

Chapter 9
Frankenstein in prison

That day, Elizabeth agreed to marry Frankenstein. I was happy in their happiness, but also a little sad because I was in love with Elizabeth myself.

Then Frankenstein told his father about his plans to take up scientific work again – in a hut in the Arve valley. Old Frankenstein was glad about that and about the plans for the marriage in November. But Elizabeth knew that Victor and I were not telling the whole truth. She felt that she was left out, and this hurt her.

The hut was away from the road, hidden by trees, and near a fast-flowing stream running down to the Arve. Frankenstein settled down there, and I brought his supplies. Some of them came from men of a very unpleasant kind, and I did not like taking them to the hut.

We knew that Elizabeth and old Frankenstein were safe: although we never saw him, it was clear that the Monster was watching the hut.

Elizabeth often asked what Frankenstein's work was.

"I'm not a scientist like Victor," I used to answer. "I don't know what it is about."

She did not like that answer, but Frankenstein would not let me tell her the truth.

By the end of October, the New Woman was ready. For the first time, I went into the work-room and saw her.

"Make her as ugly as myself," the Monster had said. She was horrible.

The weather remained unusually sunny. Frankenstein waited for the lightning. The waiting gave him time to think; and doubts crowded into his mind.

I returned to Belrive, promising to return to the hut if the weather changed. This time Elizabeth said very little about Frankenstein and the hut. After two days, I went to Geneva to do some business for old Frankenstein. At the town gates I met a friend.

"What are you doing here, Clerval?" he said. "Frankenstein is in prison here, and they say you are mixed up in it too."

"In prison?" I said. "For what?"

"Don't you know? He killed someone, they say. A boy who was fishing in the Arve found a human leg in the water. So the authorities sent men to search, and they found an arm in a stream near a hut, and Frankenstein getting ready to leave."

I hurriedly rode back to Belrive. Questions raced through my brain.

Frankenstein's wait, I decided, had made him change his ideas. He saw that it was wrong to give life to yet another monster. He had destroyed the body and thrown the pieces in the stream.

"But the Monster will find out," I thought. "Old Frankenstein and Elizabeth are in the greatest danger."

When I reached the house I jumped off my horse, and did not even stop to tie it to the usual tree before running inside. By then I felt sure that something frightful had already happened. But as I entered the sitting room, what did I see? Old Frankenstein sitting in his favourite window-seat quietly reading a book. So the Monster had not reached the house, after all. There was still time to prepare.

In as few words as possible I told the old gentleman about Victor being in prison. He had already suffered so much, and for a minute I feared that this bad news would make him ill. However, he seemed to take it in without too much excitement, and I went on: "Victor, of course, has not killed anybody. They have made a mistake, and can prove nothing in a court of law. You will do what you can to get him out of prison. But this is not all. There is danger. I cannot tell you now what Victor has been doing. All I will say is that he has made an enemy – a powerful bloodthirsty enemy who, if he cannot destroy Victor himself, will destroy his family and friends. We must prepare ourselves for his coming; he may even be here tonight. Elizabeth must be told at once."

"Ah, my friend," said the old man, shaking his head sadly. "You have come too late. Elizabeth is not here."

"Not here?" Now it was my turn to be surprised. "Where is she, then?"

"Just after you left this morning she told me that she was going to visit Victor in his hut. She went off with our servant, Emile, at about nine o'clock."

No wonder she had been so quiet about Frankenstein and the hut! She had been planning this journey all the time. She knew that I would not take her, so she had decided to go by herself – to the hut of all places, where it was very possible that the angry Monster was waiting. I had expected the Monster to come to Elizabeth, but I had never expected Elizabeth to go to him.

There was no time to waste. While old Frankenstein got ready to go to Geneva to try to get his son out of prison, I took a fresh horse and rode back along the lake. This time I took a pistol with me. From now on it was kill or be killed.

I left the lake road at Cologny, and followed small country roads to the valley of the Arve. There was just a chance that I might meet the Monster on the way, since he would not go by the busy road that Elizabeth had taken.

54

There was still a chance that he had missed her; still a chance that she would not find the hut.

However, I did not meet the Monster on the way. And when I came at last to the edge of the wood in which the hut stood, my fears increased. Two untied horses were eating the grass. These were the horses that Elizabeth and Emile had taken. Emile would never have left them to wander like this.

I tied my own horse to a tree and went the rest of the way on foot, holding my pistol ready. As I came near the hut I stopped and listened, but there was no sound except the noise of the stream. Stepping forward, I looked in through the open window of Frankenstein's work-room.

Everything in it had been completely destroyed! Only a creature of more than human strength and more than human hate could have done such things as had been done in that room: every piece of metal bent and torn; every piece of wood broken into the smallest pieces; glass beaten to powder. Only a madman could have done it, and I tried not to think of what the angry Monster might do to a living person if this was what he did to things.

I went in and searched every room of the hut, but found nobody, dead or alive. I looked all round the outside of the hut, but still found nothing.

At first I did not see Emile lying by the side of the stream. It was not exactly that I did not see him. I just did not see him as a human shape. His arms, legs and head were so unnaturally arranged that he looked like something else. Every bone is his body must have been broken. I could see at once that he was dead, but what about Elizabeth? I went up and down the stream several times and found nothing. I searched the woods near the hut. Still nothing.

Henri looks at the destroyed work-room

I spent the rest of the afternoon looking in ever-widening circles round the hut without any success. Then, just before it began to get dark, beside a path leading out of the wood on the south I found a shoe. It was Elizabeth's. With fear in my heart I searched all round this place but found nothing else. To find nothing was best, I told myself. He must surely have carried her off alive.

Just as this thought came into my mind I heard a sound behind me. I reached for my pistol, but there was no need.

"Frankenstein!" I cried.

"Have I come too late?" he asked. Then as he saw doubt in my face, he said: "Don't be afraid. I haven't escaped. My father promised to bring me in front of the judges when the time comes, and they let me out. I don't have to tell you what happened after you left me. You know my mind. You must know what I did here. Now you must tell me what happened here since."

I told my story, short as it was. When I had finished, he took the shoe from me and held it close to his heart for a long time without speaking. He looked like an unhappy child holding on to a favourite plaything. He seemed to have lost all power to do anything.

I led the way back to the hut. It was now dark and cold. I made a fire with the bits of broken furniture and we ate the small amount of food that I had brought along. What were we to do? The trouble was that we knew nothing. Was Elizabeth alive or was she no more than a broken body lying in some dark corner of the woods? We did not know. But the hope that she was alive remained. If the Monster had meant to kill her he would surely have done it here. He must have taken her with him, either as a way of making Frankenstein begin work again on a new body, or to make her his wife. The great question was where had they gone, and to that there seemed to be no answer.

In the end we cleared a corner of the room and settled down for the night. We could do nothing until the first light of day. Perhaps even then we could do nothing.

Chapter 10
The end of the Monster . . . and Frankenstein

We were tired, but we did not sleep. As well as the unanswerable questions that raced around our minds all night the sound of thunder far away wakened old fears. The fine weather which had been the cause of Frankenstein's deciding to end the experiment was breaking up at last.

Cold and hungry, and with arms and legs that did not seem to want to bend, we went out at first light and led our horses to drink from the stream. Then we started along the path where I had found the shoe the day before. All we knew was that the Monster had passed that way about sixteen hours earlier. He could be anywhere by now.

We stopped and thought, and decided to continue along the path. We had no better ideas. We followed it out of the woods to the south-west until we came to a place where it went two ways. One way turned back towards the upper Arve valley, and the other continued towards the Salève. Had he gone up the Arve to Chamonix and the great glacier above? It made sense. He knew we could never follow him through the snows of the highest mountains at this time of the year. As we stopped there, trying to decide which path to take, I noticed something lying a little way along the second of the two paths. I got down from my horse and walked over to pick it up. It was Elizabeth's other shoe! Frankenstein came up, took it in his hands and turned it over doubtfully.

"Well," I said, "aren't you pleased? Isn't it a piece of luck? Just when we need to know which way they went, we find this."

"Exactly," my friend replied. "Just when we need to know. Luck? I'm not so sure."

"Then it must be Elizabeth's doing," I said. "She's trying to show us the way."

Frankenstein shook his head. "I think the truth is less simple than you think, I believe both these shoes were dropped by the Monster."

"By the Monster?" I cried. "But why should he want us to know where he has gone?"

"Don't you see? To draw us into his power," was Frankenstein's answer. "I think he wants to destroy all three of us. He has Elizabeth, and he is using her to catch us. That shoe was lying right in the middle of the path. It was just too easy."

I did not believe him then. But when at the next place where the path went two ways we found a handkerchief hanging from a branch of a tree, I began to think my friend might be right. I kept my hand on my pistol from that time on.

It was about ten o'clock when we stopped to rest under the shadow of the Salève. It was not clear where we were meant to go from there. If the Monster was looking for a wild place to live in, he would not choose the Salève. This was not a place of snow and ice, but pleasant grassland lying on top of great white cliffs.

Frankenstein had said little that morning; but there was a look on his face that told me more than words could ever tell. He would not rest now until he had destroyed his creature – or until he himself was destroyed.

More thunder sounded, much nearer now. I looked up to the mountain, now unusually clear in the still, heavy air that waited for the coming storm. Something was moving along the edge of the cliff. "Too big for a man, or an

The Monster with Elizabeth on the edge of the cliff

animal," I said, pointing.

Frankenstein looked up. "But not for a monster carrying a girl," he said. "You see, he is right on the edge of the cliff where he can be seen against the sky. Clever. He knows we are here, and means us to follow him."

We rode on towards a break in the cliff, where it was possible to climb up to the top by a rocky path. There we left our horses and started climbing. Usually the Monster would have been able to move much faster than us, but even he must have felt the weight of Elizabeth, and when we got to the top we found ourselves not so far behind him.

"If he saw us when we were below, why did he not attack us when we were coming up the cliff? Why is he racing on like this?"

"He still wants to lead us on," Frankenstein replied. "He is making for the highest point of the cliff. When he gets there he will throw her down. And if we are there to see him do it, the greater will be his pleasure."

The storm was about to break over us. As we pushed on higher and higher over the rough grass, the first few heavy drops of rain began to fall. Every few minutes a flash of lightning lit up the shape of the Monster, half carrying, half pulling Elizabeth nearer and nearer to the place he had chosen for her death. He was tired now, and as we began to get closer, he kept looking back. Evil burned in his eyes, and his hair – made wet by the now heavy rain – hung down over his face like oily rope.

Frankenstein and I were climbing side by side. Since I was on the cliff side, I gave as much attention to the placing of my feet as to what the Monster was doing. One careless step on the wet rock meant a fall of a hundred metres and certain death.

We were very close behind him when the first lightning struck the high rocks in front. I remember smelling that strange burning smell that it gives off when close. The Monster stopped, and I thought at first that he was blinded by the flash. But then he suddenly turned to face us, holding Elizabeth in his arms.

I pulled out my pistol from inside my coat where I had been keeping it dry. I just had time to see that I could not possibly use it without putting Elizabeth in danger, when all at once the Monster raised her high above his head and threw her at me with all his strength.

If her body had struck me any higher, it would have carried me over the edge; which, of course, was what the Monster was trying to do. As it happened, only my feet went over, and I found myself hanging there with my arms around Elizabeth's neck. She put her arms round my neck, and there we were, both for the minute helpless; she lying on the edge, and me hanging over it. I remember listening to the sound of my pistol falling from rock to rock, until at last it went off with a loud noise somewhere near the bottom of the cliff.

"Hold on! Hold on!" I cried, wildly trying to find a foothold in the rock. I could not see what Frankenstein and the Monster were doing. Nor did I care. The most important thing in the world for me just then was to get one leg over the edge of the cliff. I did it. After that it was not hard to get my whole body up. As I lay there getting my strength back, I saw that Frankenstein and the Monster were fighting further along on the edge of the cliff. The rock beneath their feet was wet with the blood that poured from a wound in the Monster's chest. It had been made by a knife in Frankenstein's hand. However, the Monster's own huge hand had closed over his, and with a sudden movement the Monster tore the knife from him. He raised it high above his head. For the first time I saw real joy on his face. I turned my head away. I could not see my friend die.

There was a blue flash, and then I could see nothing.

I woke up to pain and the smell of burning. This time it was not just the smell of burnt air. My coat was on fire. I tore it off, and threw it on the ground and put the fire out with my feet. One side of my face hurt, and as I put my hand up to feel it, I found that some of my hair was burnt. All round me the grass was brown and smoking. I had stood closer to death than I had ever stood before, and I thanked God that I was still alive.

Elizabeth was lying at my feet. Her clothes were also burnt, but the heavy rain had already put out the fire. I raised her to her knees, and as I held her body to mine I felt her heart beating. She was alive.

But what about Frankenstein and the Monster?

I turned to where I had last seen them. One blackened mass was all that was left of their bodies. Together in death, creator and creature could no longer be separated.

It was some time before I could work out what had happened. The knife which the Monster had raised to drive into Frankenstein's body had drawn down the lightning upon him. That same force of nature which had created him had destroyed him.

Shaking myself free from the waking dream that held me, I pulled Elizabeth to her feet, and hand in hand we hurried down the mountain, not stopping until we reached the frightened horses below.

Blackened, burnt and wet to the skin, we rode to Geneva in complete silence.

The end of the Monster and Frankenstein

For some, at least, this strange, unhappy story ended well. Although we did not know it, as we rode through the rain that day, happier days were waiting for Elizabeth and me.

The death of Victor was a heavy loss to bear, whether he was remembered as a friend, or a lover or a son. Old Frankenstein took the news badly, as one might expect. But he was strong in mind and body. He lived not only long enough to give Elizabeth and me his blessing when we got married, but also to see our first son given the name of Victor.

I am an old man now – as old as Frankenstein's father was then. Like him, too, I have lived to see the death of a much-loved wife. Since it cannot be long before I follow her, I have set this story down, as I promised at the beginning, so that it will not die with me.

As for the secret of creating life, that died with Frankenstein. Perhaps, as scientists learn more, that secret will one day be rediscovered. But by that time I shall be dead. And I think I shall not be sorry.

Questions

Questions on each chapter

1 The young Frankenstein
    1 What is the name of the narrator ("I", "me", "my", etc) of the story?
    2 Who was Henri's best friend at school?
    3 What country did Elizabeth come from?
    4 What happened to the tree below the Salève?
    5 Which university did Victor Frankenstein go to?

2 What Frankenstein had made
    1 Who went to Ingolstadt to see Frankenstein?
    2 What did he hear when he rang the bell?
    3 What did Henri notice about the inside of the front door?
    4 What was the smell in Frankenstein's work-room like?
    5 What was in the bath?

3 Creating life
    1 What science had become Frankenstein's chief study?
    2 Frankenstein had made a body. What was he waiting for?
    3 Where had he got the parts for the body?
    4 What were Frankenstein's plans for training the perfect man?
    5 What sound did they hear through the open window?

4 We seem to fail
    1 What did Frankenstein carry up to the roof?
    2 What did he join to it?
    3 What power did Frankenstein want to use?
    4 "The experiment has failed." What made Frankenstein say that?
    5 What did Frankenstein and Henri do after that?

5 *The Monster*

   1 What was the dark shape that came into the bedroom?
   2 Why did the Monster run out of the house?
   3 Where did he run to?
   4 Why did nobody believe the gatekeeper?
   5 Where did Henri see the Monster?
   6 Who told Henri about the Monster's goodness?
   7 Who told him about the Monster's cleverness?
   8 What did Henri tell the de Lacys about Frankenstein?
   9 What happened to the de Lacys' house?
  10 What happened to William?

6 *Murder!*

   1 What happened to Justine?
   2 Who killed William?
   3 Why couldn't Frankenstein save Justine?
   4 Why did Frankenstein search for the Monster *before* Justine's death?
   5 Why was he going to search for the Monster *after* her death?

7 *We find the Monster*

   1 Where did the Monster come to Frankenstein and Henri?
   2 What happened when the Monster went to a village?
   3 What happened when Agatha de Lacy first saw him?
   4 What happened when he told Agatha of his love?
   5 What did he do to the de Lacys after that?
   6 How did he kill William?
   7 What kind of woman must Frankenstein make?
   8 What did the Monster promise to do if Frankenstein made him a wife?

8 *Elizabeth*

   1 What promise did Frankenstein make to the Monster?
   2 What did old Frankenstein talk to Victor about?
   3 What did Elizabeth see at her window?
   4 Where did Frankenstein plan to work?
   5 What did he want Henri to do?

9 *Frankenstein in prison*
  1 Old Frankenstein was glad about two things. What were
   they?
  2 What did the boy find in the river?
  3 Where had Elizabeth gone?
  4 What had the Monster done to the hut?
  5 What had he done to Emile, the servant?
  6 Where did Henri find one of Elizabeth's shoes?
  7 Who came to the hut?

10 *The end of the Monster ... and Frankenstein*
  1 How did they find the right path?
  2 What did they see on the edge of the cliff?
  3 What did the Monster do with Elizabeth?
  4 Where was the knife when the lightning struck?
  5 Who was young Victor?

Questions on the whole story

These are harder questions. Read the Introduction, and think hard about the questions before you answer them. Some of them ask for your opinion, and there is no fixed answer.

1 What does the power of lightning do in *three* parts of this story?

2 The Monster:
   a Henri sees him *four* times in this story. Say what happens each time:
     1 In Ingolstadt
     2 In the forest near Ingolstadt
     3 On the Mer de Glace
     4 On the cliffs of the Salève
   b Why did Henri fail to shoot the Monster?

3 What was Victor Frankenstein trying to do at the time of his death? Why?

4 Consider these happenings:
   1 The death of the de Lacys
   2 The death of William Frankenstein
   3 The death of Victor Frankenstein
   and answer these questions about each of them:
     a Did the Monster want it to happen?
     b Why did it happen?

5 What is your opinion of Henri Clerval's character? Does the story have the right ending for him?

6 Victor Frankenstein says in Chapter 3: "I have plans to take him to live in a place far from the spoiling example of man, where training will bring out his natural goodness."
   a Why did he not follow those plans?
   b Do you think he would have been successful?
   c Can you imagine the result?

7 Why do you think film-makers use the Frankenstein story so often?

New words

authorities
  people who rule
brain
  the mind; grey matter
  inside the head that we use
  when we think
disgusting
  very nasty, making one feel
  sick
experiment
  a scientist's work, finding
  the result of doing certain
  things
flash
  a sudden bright light
French
  of France
glacier
  a slow-moving river of ice
horror
  a feeling of great fear
human
  of men, women and
  children
kite
  paper or cloth over a very
  light arrangement of wood;
  we make it fly on the end of
  a long string

lightning
  a flash of electricity in the
  sky in a storm
monster
  a very large, strange and
  frightening animal or
  person
publish
  print and sell books: a
  publisher arranges for
  books to be printed and
  sold
thunder
  the sound of an electric
  storm
university
  a place of learning that
  one goes to after leaving
  school